W9-DBQ-278

"It's almost bedtime,"
said William.
"I'm going to hide."

"It's almost bedtime,"
said William's mother and father.

WILLIAM, WHERE ARE YOU?

by Mordicai Gerstein

Crown Publishers, Inc.   New York

"He's not out here," said the sparrow.

"Maybe he's under the dining room table."

'Are you
under the
dining room
table,
William?"

"William's
not under there,"
said the cat.

"Maybe he's behind the couch."

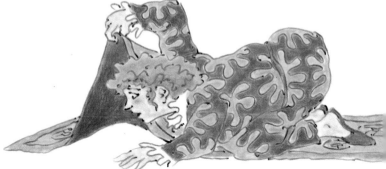

"Maybe he's
in the hall closet."

"Maybe he's under the kitchen sink."

"Are you under the kitchen sink, William?"

"He's not under here," said the mouse.

"Maybe he's
in the chandelier."

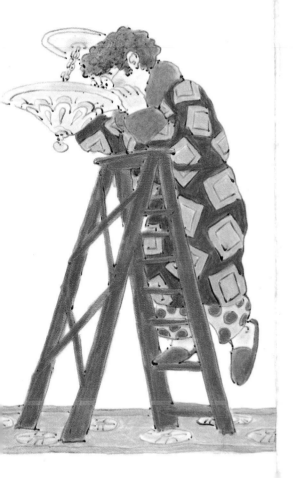

"Maybe he's in the laundry basket."

Are you in
the laundry
basket,
William?"

"He's not
in here,"
said the kittens.

"Maybe he's behind the drapes."

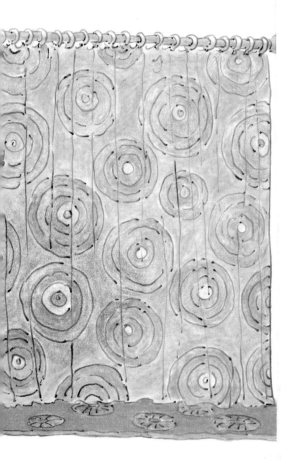

"Maybe he's in the bathtub."

"Are you
in the bathtub,
William?"

"William's
not in here,"
said the turtle.

"Maybe he's under his bed."

"Are you
under your
bed, William?"

"NO!"
said William's
baby sister.

"I'M IN BED!"
said William.
"I knew you'd *never*
look for me here."

"Good night," said William's mother and father and sister and all the animals.

"Good night,"
said William.

Copyright © 1985 by Mordicai Gerstein
All rights reserved. No part of this book may be reproduced or transmitted in any form or by any
means, electronic or mechanical, including photocopying, recording, or by any information
storage and retrieval system, without permission in writing from the publisher. Published by
Crown Publishers, Inc., One Park Avenue, New York, New York 10016 and simultaneously in
Canada by General Publishing Company Limited. Manufactured in Japan

Library of Congress Cataloging in Publication Data   Gerstein, Mordicai. William, where are you?
Summary: At bedtime William hides and his parents look for him inside and outside the house.
1. Children's stories, American. [1. Hide-and-seek—Fiction. 2. Bedtime—Fiction] I. Title.
PZ7.G325Wi 1985 [E] 84-21479 ISBN 0-517-55644-8 First Edition 10 9 8 7 6 5 4 3 2 1